Totally Twins

Musical Mayhem

The Fabulous Diary
of Persephone Pinchgut

Sweet Cherry
Publishing

Author
Aleesah Darlison

Illustrator
Serena Geddes

Published by Sweet Cherry Publishing Limited
Unit E, Vulcan Business Complex
Vulcan Road
Leicester, LE5 3EB
United Kingdom

www.sweetcherrypublishing.com

First published in the UK in 2016
ISBN: 978-1-78226-295-4

Published by Sweet Cherry Publishing in 2016

First published in Australia in 2010 by
New Frontier Publishing

Musical Mayhem: The Fabulous Diary of Persephone Pinchgut

Series: Darlison, Aleesah. Totally twins.
Target Audience: For primary school age.
Other Authors/Contributors:
Geddes, Serena.

Designed by Nicholas Pike

Printed and bound in India by Thomson Press India Ltd.

To my family.
Aleesah Darlison

To Nerelle and Shantelle for reminding
me that as annoying as sisters can be,
they will always be your best friends.
Serena Geddes

Sunday 7 February. 12:22 pm

On my bed.

Hi, and welcome to the sometimes-cool, sometimes-crazy world of Persephone River Pinchgut. (That's me!)

This is my first ever entry in my first ever personal diary. Totally brilliant, huh? Plus, I'm writing with a brand new purple gel pen, which is so silky smooth!

BTW (by the way), Mum and Portia don't know I've started a diary so this is TOP SECRET. If they did know, they'd snoop for sure, especially Portia. I've never kept a secret from her before. Why? Because she's my identical, twin sister.

I thought that seeing as how I'm nearly eleven,

and getting older and more mature by the second, that maybe I should start doing things - well, a thing - on my own. I'm 'testing the water', as Gran would say. So, keeping a diary should be one thing I can do on my own. Well, that's the plan. So, here goes.

TEN TOTALLY TERRIFIC THINGS YOU NEED TO KNOW ABOUT ME

1. My birthday is May 29.

2. My star sign is Gemini: the twins. Spooky coincidence or what?

3. I'm in Year Five at Heartfield Heights Primary School.

4. My favourite things are hanging out with my friends, swimming, collecting stationery (including gel pens, of course) and reading awesome books.

5. My favourite food is cheese and lettuce sandwiches (on white bread), followed closely by chocolate.

6. My two best friends in the whole world are Caitlin and Jolie.

7. My number one pet hate is being compared to Portia all the time! Yawn.

8. My favourite colour is purple.

9. My favourite room in the house is my bedroom – or at least my clean side of it, but definitely not Portia's messy side.

10. When I grow up, I'm going to be an archaeologist in Egypt. Not only do I find all things Egyptian totally fascinating, I love the idea of digging up ancient jewels that haven't been seen by human eyes for thousands of years.

Uh-oh, Mum's calling me for lunch. We're having vegetarian lasagne (one of Mum's better-tasting meals). TTYL (talk to you later).

Sunday 7 February. 1:04 pm.
Hiding on the front porch while
Mum and Portia do the washing up.

Phew, that was close! I had to sit on my diary while Portia came running around the corner like a maniac looking for her strawberry lip gloss.

Well, I've given you the run-down on me. Here's the goss on my family situation. I live with my mum, Skye, and my twin sister, Portia. Portia's middle name is Flame. I'm River, she's Flame: water and fire. Get it? I think Mum was trying to be clever when she named us.

11

MY MUM

Mum has always been into totally out-there things. When she was pregnant with Portia and me she was into Greek mythology and Shakespeare. That's what I'm guessing anyway. Why else would she name me after the Goddess of the Underworld and Portia after the heroine in Shakespeare's play *The Merchant of Venice*? According to Mum, Shakespeare is the greatest playwright of all time. I have my doubts.

Last year, Mum was into reiki, which is a way of healing people by touching them with your hands, and iridology, which is studying the patterns and colours of someone's eyes to determine if they are healthy or not.

Before that, she was into feng shui, which is a Chinese way of organising your home for harmony and positive energy (whatever that means). You wouldn't think our house was feng shui. It's totally messy because Mum and Portia leave their stuff everywhere, but Mum has spent ages ensuring we have perfect chi. It will bring us good fortune any day now, or so Mum says.

At the top of mum's current list are yoga and laughter therapy. She teaches classes for both in our living room so we usually have stacks of people here. All her students adore her. The problem is, Mum is often so busy with her alternative therapies that Portia and I barely get to see her.

MY DAD

Dad is very different to Mum. He is not into the 'alternative lifestyle'. He is totally conventional and (don't tell him I said this) totally unadventurous. The most adventurous thing he has ever done is move to England - and that was two years ago after his split with Mum!

At first, he wasn't planning on moving there. He only went to 'sort himself out' and 'reconnect with family'. Dad's family is originally from England so he wanted to trace his family tree. Apparently, when people get oldish like Dad, that's what they do. You know, they try to work out where they've come from so they can figure out where they're going to.

Anyway, when Dad got to England he found several well-decayed ancestors, a new life and a new wife, so he stayed.

Dad doesn't phone much because it's too expensive. Portia and I have tried talking to him on Facebook and email, but he doesn't write often enough for a proper conversation. I want to get Skype so we can talk via video, but we'd have to buy a camera because our computer is so old that it doesn't have a built-in one. Mum refuses to do that because it costs money. She can be stingy sometimes.

MY GRAN

Speaking of elderly things, my gran is really cool and not like most other grannies because she doesn't cook, she doesn't knit and she can't stand cats. Instead, she's into bungy jumping and cycling and swimming in the surf, even in the middle of winter. Brrrr!!!! Her skin is ultra-brown and wrinkly and Mum is always telling her to be sun smart, but it never sinks in. Gran does exactly what she wants to do.

Gran's a travel writer so she is away a lot. She's actually holidaying in the Maldives at the moment, researching her next travel book. Lucky thing!

MY TWIN SISTER, PORTIA

Now we come to Portia, my twin - not my clone like some people say. Obviously, though, because we are identical she does look like me. We have the same sunshine-and-honey hair down past our shoulders with soft curls at the back (which Portia is forever flicking about); the same 'crystal-green cat's eyes', as Mum calls them; and the same pointy elbows and skinny fingers.

Except for a teardrop-shaped mole on my left cheek, we look exactly the same. Oh, and most of the time I wear my hair in a ponytail (with four bobby pins on either side so nothing escapes), while Portia wears hers out. She says it's more flattering like that. I just find a ponytail tidier.

On the inside, though, we're totally different.

For instance, we never agree on things like keeping our room tidy, or what clothes to buy so we can share them, or what sort of cake we like best. (I like chocolate, Portia likes vanilla.)

That's why Mum calls us 'polar opposites', and why Portia calls me winter and herself summer. 'You're dark and serious,' she always says, 'while I'm airy and light.'

I tell her, 'Whatever.' But I think she has a point.

Monday 8 February. 3:45 pm.

My bedroom.

DISASTER has struck and you're so totally not going to believe what's happened. It's so incredibly bad I don't know what to do.

Okay, so are you ready for it?

This can't be happening. Deep breath. Here goes.

Our class has to perform an end-of-term musical!

That's right, a musical. Honestly, I'd rather use a public toilet or public shower without flip-flops. Why? Because I have zilcheroonie singing ability. I'm totally without tune. The very thought of singing in front of a real, live audience with all those eyes on me makes me shake like a skinny-minnie greyhound on a windy day.

We only started drama this year and I only chose it because Portia made me. No-one mentioned anything about singing. This is extra, extra bad news. I just know I'm going to make a total gooper of myself with my horrendous cat-getting-its-tail-pulled singing!

Hang on. Intruder alert!

I'm back. Still in my bedroom.

Another close call! I had to stash my diary under my quilt while Portia scratched around the room looking for her strawberry lip gloss. Maybe if she kept her side tidy she'd know where things were.

Portia, of course, is ecstatic about the musical. Not only is she already Miss Tamarind's (our drama teacher) favourite, she's also a fabulous singer. Wouldn't you know it? Everything Portia is, I'm not.

That's why, when Miss Tamarind delivered the news, unlike me, Portia was oozing with joy and shouted, 'That's so cool, Miss T!' Even the boys were excited. 'Awesome!' Flynn said. 'I'm the best singer.'

Some kids actually chanted (yes, chanted), 'Mu-si-cal! Mu-si-cal!'

Miss Tamarind grinned and said she was glad we were all so keen.

I wasn't. I was horrified and sat slumped to one side like a crumbling sandcastle, thinking, 'I can't do this. I can't sing.'

Miss Tamarind's crinkle-look, peasant skirt swished as she strode around the room dropping lime-green handouts about the musical onto our desks. She took great delight in telling us auditions were next Tuesday. Next Tuesday! Can you believe it?

Anyway, I stared at the page Miss Tamarind

handed me - without reading anything because I was in total shock - while a tight feeling gripped my chest. Miss Tamarind looked at me as if my face was lime-green too. It probably was. I did feel sick. She asked me if everything was okay and made a big deal of telling me how excited 'my twin' was and that she had thought I would be too.

Now, what Miss Tamarind and most other people don't realise is that just because Portia and I look the same it doesn't mean we think the same or that we are the same. We are individuals, but explaining that is all too hard sometimes.

So, instead, I grimace-smiled back at Miss Tamarind. You know, like when someone steps on your toe and it completely kills, but you smile because you're trying to be polite and pretend you can't feel it.

'I'm fine,' I said.

Miss Tamarind smiled knowingly and moved onto the next desk where she dropped another lime-green bomb. Her next piece of startling (Not!) news was that Principal Moody had agreed to let the school band play on the night.

All I hope is that they play ear-splittingly loud so when I sing they drown me out.

Hayley, a totally talented flute player, asked Miss Tamarind what would happen if you were in the band.

'Aha,' I thought, 'maybe I can take up the trombone and avoid singing that way.'

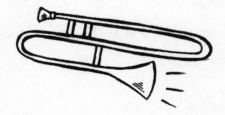

'The band will have to do without some of its players because I want our entire class on stage,' she said, dashing my plan.

Jacob asked, 'What if you can't sing?'

Good question, Jacob!

'It's not important if you can't sing,' said Miss Tamarind. (Not to her, maybe.) 'What matters is that you give it a go. I'm not looking for the next Idol. I'm looking for students who will embrace the experience.'

Please! I wanted to tell Miss Tamarind that having a good time and singing didn't necessarily go together for some people, but I didn't think she would have been interested. This was her brilliant idea, after all. Plus, with everyone else so pumped about the musical I would have sounded like a total wet blanket if I'd complained.

So, instead, I tried catching Portia's eye to

send her a SECRET SIGNAL of distress. She was too busy staring into space with a dreamy look in her eyes and a twitchy smile on her lips to see me. She was probably fantasising that she was some famous singer performing in a concert or skipping up on stage to receive an international singing award in front of millions of screaming fans, or something equally celebrity-like and singer-ish, which would be totally Portia's thing.

I'm back. I had to grab a cheese and lettuce sandwich (on wholegrain, unfortunately) because I was starving. White bread is heaps yummier, but Mum is dead against processed flour. She says it contains toxic bleaches and blocks your intestines. Appetising!

BTW, Mum's still not home. Wonder where she is? She's probably out stocking up on non-toxic, non-intestine-blocking products at the organic food store. Portia's in the lounge room watching music videos again. She's probably getting pointers for her upcoming performance.

So, where was I? Oh, yeah, Heartfield Heights Musical.

Anyway, while I was freaking out over Miss

Tamarind's announcement about the musical, Caitlin told Portia, 'You should try out for the lead. You're a brilliant singer.'

MY BESTIE, CAITLIN

Caitlin is one of Portia's and my best friends. She's in the choir with Portia and Jolie, our other bestie. We're a gang of four. We sit together in class and spend every recess and lunchtime together. Sometimes other girls hang out with us - it's not like we're snobs or anything - but basically four is a good number for us. Four is my favourite number, BTW. It's just perfect don't you think?

Well, when Caitlin said that, Portia flicked her hair and admitted she'd love to be the princess.

'Who wouldn't?' said Caitlin. 'You gad about in gorgeous dresses, you wear sparkly tiaras and you get to kiss the prince.'

'Or the frog,' I said.

Caitlin giggled. 'Oh, admit it
Perse, playing a princess would
be awesome.'

I rolled my eyes and mumbled something
even I didn't hear, while Portia said she wasn't
sure about kissing any boys. She wanted to know
if Miss Tamarind would make someone do that.
I was adamant I wasn't going to kiss anyone.
I've seen what boys get up to at lunchtime and
it's certainly not hygenic. Imagine the germs
you could catch!

Jolie asked me which part I wanted and I said
none because I couldn't sing very well. Portia
snorted and said I couldn't sing at all and that
if Jolie and Caitlin heard me they'd not only be
shocked and horrified but terrified as well.

Then Portia kept going on about how bad I

was until I got so angry my ears started to burn, like they always do when I get cranky.

Silently I counted to ten, doing the ujjayi breathing Mum taught me in yoga. Slow. Deep. Rhythmic. Mum says calming your breath quietens your mind.

Haaaa…

'It won't hurt to give it a go.' Jolie's worried eyes flicked from Portia to me and back again.

Haaaa…

Portia snort-giggled like a pig in a laughing competition. 'Oh, yes it will,' she said. 'It'll hurt our ears!'

There was no way I could quieten my mind with Portia carrying on like that, so I hissed, 'Stop it!' She just raspberried me, which was so infuriating. Luckily the recess bell rang, saving me from further humiliation. I hate losing my cool like that. I wish I hadn't, but I couldn't help it. Portia has an irritating habit of knowing exactly how to push my buttons.

The moment the bell rang, Portia, Caitlin and Jolie jumped up, not bothering to pack up their pencils or books, which is typical. They're so messy.

'Bags being first at skipping!' Portia said.

'You're always first,' Caitlin grumbled.

'Well, I'm second,' Jolie said.

They bounded out of the classroom, giggling and chattering and totally forgetting about me. They hadn't even bothered to notice how I was feeling or what I was going through as a non-singer being forced to perform in a musical. It was like they didn't care about me at all.

By now, I was feeling totally sorry for myself and wondering what to do. I was so afraid of singing on stage that I was almost in tears. To stop myself, I thought about our maths lesson coming up after recess. Bad idea! It only made me more miserable, if that's at all possible!

So, trying not to think about musicals or mathematics, I slowly tidied my desk, tucked my chair in and trudged outside.

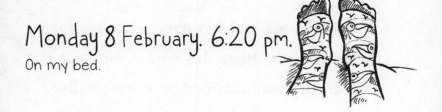

Monday 8 February. 6:20 pm.
On my bed.

Portia is a total pelican. I thought she was TOTT (totally over the top) at school, hassling me about my singing. Now she's being a pain at home too.

Mum strolled in a while ago, late as usual and bursting with news about her new art teacher at college, Mr Divine, who'd been 'so inspiring'.

'I have to get something onto canvas this instant,' she told us as she made a beeline for her sanctuary, otherwise known as her art studio.

So, no time for a deep and meaningful discussion with Mum about the day's disastrous events.

Mum's 'art studio' sounds quite posh, but in reality it's just a screened-off section of our wobbly veranda which surrounds our sagging weatherboard cottage. It's so ancient that if it were human it would need to be hospitalised.

Our house is certainly no castle, except that it might be as decrepit as one of those crumbly old 13th century ones in Scotland - only much, much smaller. And damper. And cheaper. You could probably fit our whole house into a proper castle's hall closet. Oh, you get the picture.

Seriously, though, our house is so decrepit you would feel sorry for it. There are about a gazillion holes in the tin roof. When it rains we have to set out buckets to catch the drips. I hate all the buckets sitting about and the constant splish splosh of water. It's so irritating and utterly annoying, not to mention wet.

After Mum went to her studio, I snuck in to watch her. She lit an incense stick (musk peach, which she always says helps her focus) and slid a blank canvas onto her easel. Then she began painting with her usual energy and intensity. Portia is so like her. Both of them are incredibly messy so it's best to stand back when they're doing something. Way back.

Mum was painting with this bright, egg yolk colour she'd mixed, and some creams and browns. As usual, it was hard to tell what she was painting because Mum's a totally abstract painter. Understanding her paintings can be difficult because they have hidden meanings. You never know if what you're seeing is what you're meant to see, if you know what I mean.

At least this one looked happy. For ages after Dad left, Mum's paintings were always black or grey or, if she was in an ultra-good mood, murky blue. Since she's taken up laughter therapy she's been better. Now she paints with colour: mostly.

Just finished watching mum paint.

I'm back. I had to slip out to the kitchen and nick the last cookie before Portia got to it. Now, to continue, while I was quietly watching Mum paint with the egg yolk colour, Portia - with no regard for anyone's personal space - came in and flopped into the hammock, one leg hanging over the side and scuffing the floorboards with her sneaker as she swung back and forth, munching a homemade organic, oatmeal cookie. Which, as I mentioned earlier, I'm now eating the last one of, BTW!

'Too close, Portia!' Mum warned.

Portia kept swinging. Does she ever get the message?

'How was school?' This is Mum's standard question.

I could tell she wasn't interested. Her tongue was poking out the corner of her mouth and her eyes were glued to her canvas.

As I nibbled my cookie (catching the crumbs, unlike Portia), I told her I got an A in geography. Of course, Portia had to tell Mum she got an A+. Show-off! Then she told Mum about the musical and went on about how great it was going to be.

Yawn! I wasn't only thinking this, I did it about ten times while I listened to Portia rabbit on. When she finally finished talking, Mum took a while to answer because she was still dabbing away.

'Hmmm. That sounds good; if you like musicals.'

Which is my point exactly. I hate musicals!

Mum wiped her forehead with the back of her hand, leaving behind a streak of orange paint. Portia shot me a cheeky SECRET SIGNAL of silence, then told Mum she was trying out for the lead and was going to be the star of the show.

I know she's the teacher's pet and everything, but stacks of other girls could play the princess. I didn't say anything. What was the point?

Mum made a few more dabs. After a while, she seemed to remember we were there and asked me whether I had my eye on a role.

I squirmed. 'You know I can't sing. Portia's so much better than me.'

Portia flicked her hair and nodded in agreement.

'I think you sing beautifully,' Mum said.

I knew she was fibbing because she tucked her hair behind her ear as she spoke. She always does that when she lies.

'If you'd prefer not to sing, perhaps you could help out backstage,' she suggested.

'Miss T's got that all covered,' Portia said, swinging the hammock closer to Mum's easel.

'She wants everyone on stage, even Perse. Plus, get this, for the ballroom scene we're using a chandelier and a staircase.'

Mum moved the easel a millisecond before Portia would have knocked it over. She kept right on painting.

'Miss Tamarind must have plenty of energy,' Mum said. 'Is she into yoga?'

'Dunno,' Portia replied, 'but she is amazing,

and pretty. She's got short, jagged hair and funky, red, toffee apple glasses, and she always wears bright, red lipstick.' By Portia's estimation, this makes her a genius.

Honestly, I think Miss Tamarind is okay and I'll admit I like her long, swishy skirts and her haircut.

However, I think I would like her a whole lot

more if she:

1. Didn't always compare me to Portia.

2. Didn't insist on referring to us as the 'Pinchgut girls' or 'the twins'.

3. Brushed her teeth after she ate garlic at lunchtime.

4. Admitted she was wrong about organising a musical and called the whole thing off!

Strangely, Portia is so totally infatuated with her beloved Miss T that she can't see her faults. They do say that love is blind though, so I guess this is a perfect example of that.

Anyway, that was when I moaned loudly about wishing we didn't have to sing.

Mum laughed. 'It's a bit hard doing a musical without the singing.'

'I know that, but I would still rather eat live spiders,' I said.

'You'd probably be better at eating live spiders than singing too,' said Portia.

Then, she sat up suddenly.

'Hey, I know. Maybe you won't have to sing. Maybe you can ask Miss T if you can play a tree or, wait I've got it, the staircase! Just wear that horrid, brown dress of yours, hold your hands like this and you'll be a perfect staircase,' she said, bending one arm in front of her at a right angle and one arm behind like an Egyptian dancer.

I didn't laugh.

'Hah-hah, hilarious,' I said. 'Anyway, it's not brown. It's caramel.'

Portia cracked up. 'It's not caramel. It's catastrophic! Honestly Perse, there's no excuse for brown clothes.'

'There's no excuse for bad manners,' I said. 'Besides, I like that dress.'

'Well, I don't,' Portia said. 'I wish you wouldn't wear it in public. People might think you're me and that I've lost all fashion sense.'

By now I was ready to strangle Portia, and would have gladly done so if Mum hadn't cut in.

'Enough!' she said, unusually cranky. 'You girls go fix yourselves some dinner. Organic noodles are nice and easy. Then do your homework. I'll be in once I've finished here.'

This just meant Portia and I were conveniently occupied while Mum continued working. Knowing Mum, she'll be in her studio forever.

Monday 8 February. 9:32 pm.
In bed.

Surprise, surprise (or should I say, no surprise) those organic noodles were totally gross. I must buy some Oreos tomorrow. Imagine, real food (and sugar) for a change.

Portia's already asleep, snoring like a deranged wombat. I wonder what she'd do if I stuffed one of her smelly socks in her mouth? After all, there's enough of them lying on the floor. Grrrr!!!!

Mum just tip - toed in. She'd been in her studio all that time. Her forehead was still streaked orange. I wasn't sure she'd been listening when we told her about the musical, but she must have heard a snippet of our conversation at least because she said I shouldn't let Portia get away with teasing me all the time.

I shrugged. 'Portia's only joking.'

Mum rested her chamomile tea on my desk and sat on the bed beside me. BTW, Mum's a herbal tea fanatic. She won't touch coffee because it gives her the shakes and keeps her up all night, so she says. Herbal tea apparently soothes her nerves by diluting toxins in the bloodstream.

Anyway, Mum went on and on, lecturing me about needing to stand up to Portia when she teases me.

'Portia's far too bossy,' she added, 'especially when it comes to her little sister.'

I couldn't help smiling at that. Portia was born two and a half minutes before me, so Mum often calls me Portia's 'little' sister.

'Now, if you did that more often, you'd feel much better,' Mum said.

'Do what?' I asked.

'Smile, or even laugh,' she said, tickling me.

After I'd finished giggling (I'm very ticklish), I told Mum I was okay about Portia and that I didn't mind her teasing me, even though I do. I just don't like talking about our Twin Troubles. Not even to Mum. That's between Portia and me.

Mum stood up and said, 'Well, as long as you're okay.'

I nodded. 'Mum, what's your painting called?'

'Sunflowers.'

I told her it was a good name, and because I couldn't stand it any longer, I told her she had paint on her forehead.

Mum smiled like she wasn't bothered at all and said, 'Thanks, sweetie. Good night.'

Tuesday 9 February. 4:42 pm.

In my room. Fuming.

FIVE THINGS I HATE MOST ABOUT MUSICALS

1. Me being in them.

2. Having to sing in front of people I know – and them laughing.

3. Having to sing in front of people I don't know – and them laughing.

4. The fact that musicals are nonsense. Who ever breaks into song for no reason – sometimes mid–sentence – in real life?

5. The possibility I might have to dance and sing at the same time, which could lead to a major accident because I am prone to clumsy episodes when I'm nervous.

You won't believe what happened today. This whole singing thing is getting worse, and it's all Portia's fault. She's gone way beyond TOTT now.

During lunch, our gang was sitting on the climbing frame munching sandwiches. As usual, Portia was perched up on the highest rung while the rest of us hung on the next rung down. BTW, we love sitting up there. It's great for seeing what's going on in the playground. More teachers should sit up there, that's for sure. They would learn heaps.

Like with everything at the moment, the conversation was focused on the musical. You'd think we were trying out for a HOLLYWOOD EXTRAVAGANZA or something. Portia sure thinks so.

'This is going to be the best musical ever,' she babbled. 'I've practically learned all the princess's lines already.'

Caitlin and Jolie chorused, 'No way!' and 'Impressive!' being the supportive and kind friends that they are.

'Show-off,' was what I was thinking, but I didn't say it.

Then Portia said, 'Hey, maybe they'll run a story in the newspaper about us.'

Caitlin puckered her forehead like she does when she's thinking or confused (or confusedly thinking). 'Why would they do that?'

'Community interest,' said Portia, as she flicked her hair and tilted her nose in the air. 'I'm going to ask Miss T to phone them.'

'You're dreaming. No-one would be interested,' I said.

She snapped right back, calling me 'Pessimistic Perse', and saying the words like they were asparagus that tasted bitter and disgusting in her mouth.

Caitlin must have sensed a twin tussle brewing because she changed the subject. 'Want to practise singing?'

Inside my head I shouted, NOOOOOOOO! because I thought it was a terrible idea, worse than calling the newspaper. But I had a mouthful of sandwich so it would have been bad manners to speak, which meant Portia and Jolie answered before I could.

'Yeah!'

Hang on. Portia's prowling.

Tuesday 9 February. 5:10 pm.
Continued.

I have returned. Portia came in searching for her lip gloss, again. If she kept it in the same spot she wouldn't lose it, would she? I've tried explaining that to her, but she doesn't get it.

She couldn't find her lip gloss anywhere and even though I could see it on the carpet beside the desk, I didn't say anything. I also kept quiet about my SECRET STASH of Oreos behind my pillow. I am perfecting the art of eating chocolate biscuits incognito. They're way too yummy to share, especially with Portia.

Anyway, enough about chocolate biscuits, back to the lunchtime singing saga.

After Caitlin suggested we sing, Portia said, 'Let's do that cool new song, *Be Mine*.'

Now, I actually adore *Be Mine*. I've heard it on the radio and it's so catchy that I can't get the tune out of my head.

But I didn't want to totally ruin the song so I sat there listening to the others sing and wishing for the trillionth time I was as good as them. No wonder they're excited about the musical. Everything's going to be okay for them.

Then, surprise of all surprises, Portia told me to join in. I nearly fell off my perch! She said it so sweetly, like the nice twin that she can be sometimes when we're alone. I thought she meant it, so I joined in:

'Hey!
I'm gon-na love you forever.
Hey!
Baby, say you'll be mine.'

None of us knew all the words, so we kept repeating the chorus (it's the best bit anyway). At first my voice was a whisper, but as I started enjoying myself I sang louder. I tried hard to make my voice sound like the other girls' voices, and I thought I was doing okay. I even remember thinking that maybe my voice wasn't so bad after all, that maybe I could sing.

Midway through the next chorus, Portia held her hands up. 'Wait, wait, wait!' Everyone stopped. Portia whispered something to Caitlin and Jolie. They glanced at me, then nodded. When I asked what was up, Portia smiled innocently and said, 'Nothing. Okay girls. From the top.'

We all sang the chorus again. Right at the end the other girls stopped dead, leaving me to sing the final line by myself,

'Baaa-byyyy saaay you'll be mii-iii-ne!'

Now that the others weren't singing, I heard how bad I was. So did they, and they BURST OUT LAUGHING.

I was so mad and embarrassed. My cheeks and ears burned bright red like they were on fire. I couldn't breathe, couldn't swallow over the lava-like lump of anger in my throat. All I could do was stare at my hands and will myself not to cry.

Of course, Portia was on a roll and pretended not to notice how upset I was. She snorted loudly (yes, she does snort a lot) and said, 'You know, Perse, if your singing was an egg it'd be R.O.T.T.E.N. Rotten!'

'Quit it!' I told her.

'You're just being a baby. I was only having fun,' she said.

'I don't like your definition of fun. What you are being is M.E.A.N. Mean.'

'You just can't see the funny side,' Portia said, 'and the funny side is you!'

Then she sang in a perfect wobbly-voiced impersonation of me,

'Baaa-byyyy saaay you'll be mii-iii-ne!'

The others laughed until tears streamed down their faces, while I sat there trying to swallow the angry flames still burning inside me. Like, I know my singing isn't great, but did Portia have to make such a big deal of it?

So, now I'm thinking the only possible solution for my current miserableness is:

CHOCOLATE, CHOCOLATE AND MORE CHOCOLATE.

Because the Oreos are all gone I'm going to sign-off so I can undertake a mammoth search for more chocolate to banish the Portia-induced blues.

I wish I'd never played that stupid singing game. Sigh.

Tuesday 9 February. 9:25 pm.

Under the covers, writing by torchlight.

I have been thinking about everything I share as a twin.

THE TOP FIVE THINGS I HATE TO SHARE

1. Birthdays.

2. A room.

3. One mum.

4. Friends.

5. A face.

The only thing truly mine is this diary.
Double sigh.

Wednesday 10 February. 7:26 pm.
Back porch, watching the stars ignite.

Tonight is yoga night, so Mum's kooky yoga friends have invaded the house again. They must be up to their meditation session because I can hear them 'ommming' and 'ahhhhing' in the lounge room. I can smell the nutmeg incense from here and it's making me sneeze!

Portia's in the kitchen playing Mastermind with Dill. Boring! I'm meant to be helping her look after him, but I can't bear being near her right now.

BTW, Dill Pickle, or Dillon Pickleton, is our totally annoying next door neighbour. He is nothing but a nuisance.

SEVEN SIGNIFICANT THINGS TO KNOW ABOUT SEVEN-YEAR-OLD DILL

1. He is not my favourite person in the whole world.

2. He is mega—fascinated with Portia and me and our identical—ness. Once, he even asked his mum if he could have a twin. So silly!

3. No matter how many times he sees us and no matter how many times we've explained how to tell us apart, Dill can never work out who is who. Whenever he spots one of us he says, 'Wait! Don't tell me. Let me guess.' Then he'll scrunch up his face trying to figure out which one of us it is. I usually let him guess, but Portia will snap, 'I'm Portia!' Then she'll stalk off and leave Dill looking like he's lost a year's supply of gummy bears.

4. Dill is an only child, which I think explains a lot, including point two.

5. He is so super-skinny he has trouble keeping his pants up, even with a belt, and especially when he runs. So funny!

6. He is obsessed with knights, like from medieval English times, and often tears around his backyard (holding his pants up with one hand) dressed as King Arthur and having pretend sword fights with his dog, Camelot. Mind you, he doesn't think I know this. But I do.

7. I can't remember the seventh most significant fact. It can't have been very significant!

Anyway, Dill's mum, Mrs Pickleton, is my mum's biggest yoga fan. She never misses a class. She wears this bright, aqua leotard with purple leggings underneath (which makes me snort with laughter every time I see her). Her hair is cut into a bob and is a bizarre fuchsia colour with purple streaks. It's true! I can't believe she pays her hairdresser to make her look like that. Adults can be so weird. Still, she's a nice person, if a little BRIGHT.

Mr Pickleton (who's a fireman and a real-life hero because he's rescued stacks of old people and small dogs from burning buildings) is working tonight, so Mum told Mrs Pickleton that Portia and I would mind Dill while she did yoga. Good one, Mum.

As it turns out, Portia is the one doing the minding, which is perfectly fine by me.

Sometimes I get so sick of Portia! We spend every hour of every day together. I wish I had my own room. Better still, I wish Dad had taken me with him when he went AWOL (absent without official leave) from our family and moved to England. I guess you can't have a midlife crisis with a kid hanging around though. That's what Gran says anyway, that Dad took off because he was having a midlife crisis.

I miss him.

If Dad was here, maybe I could talk to him about this musical, like I used to talk to him about things that were bothering me.

Hang on. I hear footsteps in the kitchen. Yoga

must be finished so they'll want their herbal teas and organic, low-fat, gluten-free (and totally tasteless) cakes. I'll have to go in, pretend to be cheery and help serve supper. That's what you call acting. TTYL.

Wednesday 10 February. 9:22 pm.
In bed. Portia snoring nearby.
Doesn't sound so sweet now, does she?

I'm so tempted to pop a bug in Portia's mouth right now. The only things stopping me are:

1. I don't want to actually touch a bug.

2. She saved me from Dill Pickle tonight.

Maybe Portia let me off the hook with Dill because she realised she went TOTT at school today. I haven't forgiven her though. That's why I ignored the SECRET SIGNAL of sorry she flashed me before going to sleep. Sometimes SECRET

SIGNALS aren't enough. Sometimes words need to be spoken. Maybe she'll say them tomorrow.

For now, though, I still have to find a way to avoid this musical. I have been racking my brain all day and have come up with some possible escape options.

TOP FIVE WAYS TO GET OUT OF SINGING IN A MUSICAL

1. Get hospitalised with (fake) laryngitis.

2. Get hospitalised with a (fake) broken leg.

3. Get hospitalised with a (fake) broken leg and (fake) laryngitis.

4. Run away from home long enough for the musical to be over, then come back. (Too obvious?)

5. Beg Mum to send me to another school (at least until the musical is over).

Thursday 11 February. 5:42 pm.
Wishing I could lock my door.

School was okay, although I'm still worried about the auditions. I couldn't concentrate in class - not even during the lesson on Ancient Egypt. What a waste of a history class!

When I came home, I flopped on my bed to wallow in anti-musical misery. Portia was at ballet practice and Mum was in her studio.

BTW, today's painting is 'Conifer Conversations' and it's entirely green. Apparently, Mr Divine inspired this piece too. I wonder if it's more than her artwork that he's inspiring because she's been rather floaty and distracted since art class on Monday.

Anyway, it was heavenly being Portia-less for a change so I thought I'd listen to some music.

Even though I can't sing, I can appreciate good songs.

I downloaded *Be Mine* onto my iPod and plugged my earphones in. Cranking up the volume, I started bopping around like all the singers in their video clips. (Well, probably nothing like them, but I can dream, can't I?) I even started miming into my iPod like it was a microphone.

Softly at first, so Mum wouldn't hear me, I started singing. Alone in my room, my voice grew louder. The dancing and singing helped me forget all the bad stuff between Portia and me. It made me HAPPY and I realised I didn't need to sing with my friends. I could sing alone in my bedroom (as badly as I wanted to) and no-one would ever know.

When the song finished, I popped the earphones out and heard clapping behind me. I turned to see Portia leaning in the doorway, barefoot and still wearing her pink ballet tutu.

'Geez, Perse,' she said, biting into an apple and revealing crunchy bits of chewed-up apple in her mouth as she spoke, 'I don't get it. How come I'm such a great singer and you're so hopeless?'

When I informed her, as politely as I could under the circumstances, that I wasn't that bad, Portia snort-laughed and said, 'You're dreadful! Boy, I can't wait to tell the gang. They'll cack themselves.'

As you can imagine, I wanted to say plenty of things to Portia (that aren't printable here), but I was so sizzling mad and was grinding my teeth together so hard that all I could manage

was a totally wordless and wolf-like, 'Grrrr!!!!'
So frustrating!

Finally, I managed to spit out, 'You can't tell them! You wouldn't dare!' Portia only giggled wickedly and said she would dare. Then she turned and skipped down the hall singing perfectly in tune, 'Hey! I'm gonna love you forever...'

Show-off!

I spent the next ten minutes imagining tonnes of sinister and unsisterly things I could have said or done to Portia. If only I'd thought of them before she left!

Hey, I know. There is one thing I can do. Because my voice is so totally hideous, so totally LOL (laugh out loud), I, Persephone River Pinchgut, do solemnly vow never to speak again.

So there!

Now I'm sitting here, staring out the window, dashing away tears that are falling as thick and fast as the rain outside. The feathery, purple flowers of the jacaranda tree that were once so pretty now blanket the grass, all brown and messy. Like my life.

Yes, it's true. My life is a dead jacaranda flower.

Soggy.

Brown.

Messy.

Now that I'm never speaking again, I'll take this diary with me everywhere so I can at least write.

Thursday 11 February. 8:00 pm.
My bedroom.

I think Mum's onto me. At dinner she asked if I was okay, felt my forehead to see if I was 'coming down with something' and muttered about being too busy to have a sick child home from school. I was surprised she even noticed me, in between Portia's forever-bubbling fountain of words.

So that Mum couldn't get too suspicious, I quickly showered and slipped in here to hide. I'm even missing *River's Town* so I don't 'accidentally' talk to Portia.

Whenever we watch *River's Town*, during the ads we discuss the storyline and whether the characters are being believable. Not wanting to be tempted into blurting something out so

Portia thinks I've forgiven her, I've decided to keep away. She owes me two apologies now, so under no circumstances can I pretend nothing's happened.

It's a shame though, because *River's Town* is my favourite TV show (except for Egyptian documentaries, which are fascinating because you learn amazing things, like the fact that the most famous Egyptian queen of all, Cleopatra, wasn't Egyptian. She was actually Greek).

Portia thinks my fascination with all things Egyptian makes me a nerd with a capital N. Double sigh!!

Portia noticed I wasn't speaking this morning and got rather shirty. She HATES being ignored. In the bathroom, she said, 'So, what's up with you?'

I kept brushing my teeth and staring into the mirror and not answering. As she brushed her hair (I think she was up to 117 strokes, but I was ignoring her so I wasn't really counting), she repeated her question, louder this time.

Calmly, I rinsed, washed my toothbrush, wiped it dry and slotted it back in the holder. Nice and neat. Then I strolled out.

'Answer me!' I heard her brush slam against the door, but I was down the hall by that time.

Portia came out and told Mum in a whiny

77

voice that I was ignoring her, but we had to leave for school so Mum shooed us out the door. I walked triple-quick time so Portia couldn't catch up to me, then scuttled straight into class when I got to school.

All morning, Mr Cleaver, our teacher, did most of the talking (he definitely fancies the sound of his own voice), so Portia wasn't able to pester me.

She hasn't mentioned the 'bedroom singing incident' to Caitlin and Jolie yet either. Maybe she's waiting for the right time to humiliate me again. Who knows?

In maths, Jolie must have noticed something was wrong because she whispered, 'You okay?'

I nodded and pretended to be captivated by the equations in my workbook, thinking I was doing some brilliant acting.

Jolie didn't buy it. 'You're not still upset about

the other day, are you? We were only joking. It didn't mean anything.'

Not to you maybe, I thought, but I couldn't say it because of my vow of silence.

'Enough chatter, girls,' Mr Cleaver said. 'Get on with your questions.'

Glad for Mr Cleaver's bossiness for a change, I bent my head and continued working. After a while, so did Jolie.

It's amazing what you learn when you're not talking. Like, today I learnt through observation that Flynn looked at Portia sixteen times in maths. Curious.

Anyway, when the lunch bell rang I scrambled up here to the library. After flicking through a book about the Great Sphinx of Egypt for the eighty-eighth time, I decided to update my diary. None of my friends have bothered looking for me, BTW.

Friday 12 February. 4:10 pm.
Hall closet, torch between my teeth.

Why the closet, you ask? Intrigue and mystery? Sadly not! I'm just escaping a drop-in from the Pickletons.

Mum picked us up in the car this afternoon, which is what you call a RARE event because she's usually too busy. Plus, she reckons we're old enough to make our own way home. I agree, but it was still nice seeing her at the gate.

I thought something must be up because she looked worried and was chewing her fingernails, which she hasn't done for ages. Fingernail chewing is a major alarm signal that something is bothering her. Being on my vow of silence though, I couldn't exactly ask.

Once we were in the car and on the way

home, I caught her watching me in the rear-view mirror so I pretended to be interested in a garbage truck driving nearby. The car windows were down and I had to hold my breath because of the stinky dead-fish-and-rotting-vegetables smell. I didn't want Mum to know that anything was wrong so I kept staring at the truck like I was in love with it. Mum soon grew distracted by the traffic and Portia's chatter so she didn't look at me again. Phew! I made it home without speaking.

When we got home, Portia dumped her bag at the door and dashed into the kitchen. Mum stumbled in behind me loaded up with art supplies.

'Portia, take your bag to your room,' she said.

'Later!' Portia called from the kitchen. 'What's to eat?'

Mum turned to me. 'Be a pet and take her

bag will you?'

I rolled my eyes, then kicked Portia's bag all the way down the hall and into our room. Mum didn't see, of course. She was too busy juggling her paint and stuff. If she had seen me she would have freaked and said something like, 'School bags cost money, you know.'

After a while, I went foraging in the kitchen for food, my diary hidden under my shirt because I was going to sneak outside and sit in the sun to write. I'd just scored the last packet of rice wheels when the doorbell rang and I heard Mrs Pickleton's ever-chirpy voice call out, 'Only me, Skye!'

This closet was my nearest escape route, so I bolted in here and left Portia to answer the door. Surely no-one will think of looking for me in the hall closet.

At least I've had time to write in peace, even though the vacuum cleaner is digging painfully into my backside.

Uh-oh. Rustling outside. Who could it be?

Dill Pickle! I should have known that little beagle would sniff me out.

'Hello? Is someone in there?' I heard his muffled seven-year-old voice on the other side of the door. When he peeked in and asked me what I was doing I told him I was working on a school project. He asked what it was on and I thought I was very clever saying, 'Cockroaches. Did you know there are over 3500 species of them?'

'No,' Dill said.

Then, he thought for a minute before asking, 'Can I help?'

'No, you can't help,' I said. 'Cockroaches are deadly poisonous to seven-year-olds.'

He squinted at me for a moment, then laughed. 'I get it. You're joking.'

I clambered out of the cupboard and brushed past him, but he called after me. 'Hey, wait! Let me guess which one you are first.'

I kept walking, saying over my shoulder, 'I'm Portia.' Dill did a little air punch and cheered, 'I knew it!' so I think I made his day, even though I didn't mean to.

Oops. Gotta go. Mum's calling me for dinner. We always eat early on Fridays because Mum has another art class and Portia and I have to look after ourselves until she gets home. It smells like spinach quiche. Hope it's minus the burnt charcoal bits this time.

Friday 12 February. 7:15 pm.
Back porch. Finally got here but, alas, no sun left!

The quiche was DELICIOUS and charcoal-free, which is always a bonus.

Something is up with Mum, for sure. She's still gnawing her fingernails (what's left of them) and painting non-stop.

After she left for her art class, I peeked in her studio. Today's painting is red. As red is the colour of love, or so I'm told, I'm wondering if Mum is in love and doesn't know it yet or hasn't bothered to tell us. Hmmm.

More importantly, what am I going to do about the musical mayhem? Each day the auditions march ever closer!

I wish Dad was here. I so need to speak to him.

I know. I'll send him an email, if I can prise Portia off the computer without speaking to her, that is.

I should be getting ready for swimming, but I have a headache and don't want to go. It's probably because I tossed and turned all night worrying about the musical.

Late last night when Mum got home she came to tuck me in and I was still awake.

'You all right, Perse?' she asked, as she sipped her chamomile tea.

She also had a book tucked under her arm. It's one she's read plenty of times called *Twin Talk* and, you guessed it, it's about raising twins. Maybe the reason for Mum's fingernail chewing is me and Portia, and not love?

'You've been quiet these last few days,' Mum said. 'Feeling all right?'

I nodded.

'So nothing's bothering you?'

Any words I wanted to say caught stubbornly in my throat. My vow of silence must prevail!

Mum kept pressing me, even asking if anything had happened at school to upset me. Not meaning to, I accidently dobbed Portia in with my eyes. She was fast asleep, snoring softly with one arm flung over her face. Mum followed my gaze.

'Is Portia bossing you around again?' she asked, turning back to me.

Pinching my lips together, I gave a rapid, wide-eyed shake of my head, doing some magnificent acting, I thought, but Mum looked doubtful.

'You know you can talk to me about things,' she said.

I nodded again, thinking I couldn't really talk to her, not always, because of her busy-ness, and not now, due to my vow of silence.

'You know you can't be good at everything, don't you?' she asked.

I nodded again, not ready to share my feelings. Like I said, the stuff between Portia and me is a twin thing. It's for us to sort out.

Mum seemed happy enough and stood up. 'Okay, we'll leave it at that. Turn out the light now.'

Still clutching *Twin Talk*, she trotted out. I flicked off the bedside lamp, then lay in the dark staring at the ceiling. That's when the tears came.

You see, it's fine for Mum to say I can't be good at everything. She doesn't know what it's like to have an identical twin who is better at everything. No-one (except maybe a twin), knows how hard it is being compared to someone else all the time, or comparing yourself to them all the time, and forever falling short. It SUCKS. Big time.

Oops. Mum's banging on the door. She's in a rush because she has to drop me off at swimming, and Portia at ballet, then race back here for a laughter therapy class. Guess I won't be getting out of it then. Luckily swimming is indoors because it's raining again.

Sunday 14 February. 5:30 pm.
Flopped on my bed.

It's Valentine's Day. Of course, there was zilcheroonie in the mailbox or on the doorstep for me, but Portia and Mum both got something.

First, there was Portia's card. She's utterly perplexed because she has no idea who sent it. It was addressed to 'Perfect Portia', and had an adorable, ginger kitten on the front, along with the words, 'Be My Valentine'. It was unsigned, though.

I have serious suspicions about who sent it (Flynn), but Portia has NO IDEA.

'If you send a Valentine's Day card,' she moaned, 'you should have the guts to sign it.' Portia hates not knowing things. I was just enjoying watching her squirm.

As for Mum, she finally introduced us to Mr Divine, and he sure lives up to his name. He is, I have to admit, good-looking for an elderly person of thirty-something. He's tall with sparkly, green eyes, springy, brown hair and a neatly trimmed goatee. I'm not sure about the goatee though, it makes him look like he's trying too hard.

He came over around lunchtime to see Mum's artwork. At least that's why Mum said he was here, but I'm not buying it. Not when she spent the ENTIRE morning doing her make-up and blow-drying her hair (more rare events).

It was also a give-away when he said 'Happy Valentine's Day', and handed her twelve (I counted them) long-stemmed red roses and a box of organic carob truffles. (He must know she's not into chocolate.)

Okay, I admit, he's not ultra-original in his choice of gifts, but I've forgiven him because the truffles were surprisingly yummy. There's only three left actually, but I won't say who ate them.

Mr Divine had to dodge the buckets set out to catch the drips from the leaking roof, which Mum was mortified about. However, he was most chivalrous and pretended not to notice, even when he tripped over the blue bucket in the hall and almost ended up head first into the green bucket in the lounge room, causing more mortification for Mum!

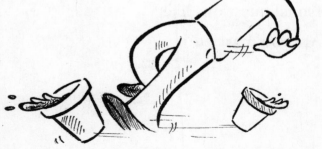

Because he asked me several direct questions, I had to break my vow of silence to answer him. I would have looked extremely rude (and he might have mistaken me for Portia) if I didn't. Plus, Mum gave me several approving looks, which are way better than her disapproving ones, so it was worth it.

Even though I'm talking again, it doesn't mean I'm ever singing again. It certainly doesn't mean I'm talking to Portia. Oh, I'll talk to her if I need to - like, 'Can you please pass the lettuce?' or, 'Can you please stop snoring?' or 'Can you please stick your head in the loo?' - but not because I want to.

Speaking of Portia, she was rather grumpy with Mr Divine and kept asking him ultra-personal questions like:

'Are you married?'

'No.'

'Where do you live?'

'Seaview, the next suburb over.'

'What do you do for a job?'

Mum jumped in here and said, 'You know what Will does, Portia, he teaches art.'

Cool as a zucchini, Portia said, 'Do you make much money doing that?'

By now, she was in severe danger of being sent to her/our room, but Mum just gave her the SECRET SIGNAL for, 'Behave or Else!'

Through it all, Mr Divine chuckled like he wasn't bothered at all. Mum kept chugging her chamomile tea and telling us to go and do something useful. Of course, we pretended not to hear!

I hope Mr Divine knows Mum has no intentions of dating. She's far too busy and probably only accepted his roses and carob truffles because he offered to arrange an exhibition at Heartfield Heights Art Gallery for her. So they're about to set a date (for the exhibition, I mean).

To his credit, Mr Divine didn't stare at Portia and me like we were freaks of nature. He didn't ask dumb questions either (important: see list on next page), like most people do when they first meet us. So, that makes me think that, overall, he's an okay guy.

Just so you know - because you never know when you might need to know - NEVER EVER ask twins the following questions:

TOP FIVE TOTALLY TRYING TWIN QUESTIONS PEOPLE ASK

1. So, you're identical twins.
   Does that mean you're sisters?

2. Which one of you is smarter?

3. Do you like being a twin? (As if we
   know what it's like not being a twin!)

4. If you have a stomach—ache,
   does your sister get it too?

5. Wait for it, it's a good one...
   Do you ever wake up and forget who you
   are and think you're the other one? As if!

School was okay, but I'm still trying to dodge the musical mayhem.

Dad finally replied to the email I sent the other day. I never mentioned Portia, BTW. I just asked what I should do about the musical. This was his reply:

Hi Perse,
Great to hear from you. Things hectic here. Opening new chocolate shop soon. Flat-out. Elle says hi.
Don't worry about musical. In a few years you won't remember it. Just give it your best shot. You'll do great.
Say hi to Portia. Miss you. Love you very much. Your loving dad.

Love, love, love! Dad's apparently full of it, but where's the non-lame parental advice?

BTW, Elle is Dad's new wife. Her full name is Eleanor Elizabeth Krankston. Her initials are EEK, so Portia and I call her EEK!

PS: Thanks for zilcheroonie, Dad.

PPS: Auditions are tomorrow and I still don't know how I'm going to escape them. Help!

Major catastrophe in progress! Wish I could throw up!

I tried getting out of school today, but Mum saw through my fake laryngitis story and sent me anyway. She said even if I was sick I'd have to go to school because she had a laughter therapy workshop to run. Nothing new there.

So, now it's lunchtime and my entire drama class - except me - is in the hall auditioning while I'm writing this.

Here's what happened. I was standing under the awning outside the hall, working up the courage to go in. It was still raining, BTW, and the smell of muddy puddles and wet cement filled the air.

I heard someone say, 'Hey, Portia!' and turned to see Flynn. I was about to correct him (in the nicest possible way, even though he made me cross by not knowing who I was), but he kept talking, saying how great the musical was going to be and asking me which part I was trying out for.

I shrugged as I stared into his caramel eyes, finding it hard to believe that Flynn MacIntosh, the cutest boy in the grade, was talking to me, Persephone River Pinchgut. Okay, minor detail, he did think I was Portia, but I still wanted to make the most of the moment. I don't mind living out a fantasy now and then.

'You'll get the lead, for sure,' Flynn said with a smile.

What a nice thing to say, I thought, except you're saying it to the wrong girl. Lost in a

Flynn-induced fantasyland, I mumbled a thank you as I watched the raindrops drip from his wet hair onto his shirt, where they made tiny wet patches.

'Yeah, like, I've heard you sing in the choir and you're awesome,' he added. Even though Flynn's compliment was meant for Portia, it still made my heart thud a little faster. He's so cute, after all.

Flynn's cheeks turned the colour of raspberries. Then he kicked an empty drink box on the ground and asked me if I liked kittens. At least I think that's what he said, but I wasn't sure.

'Pardon?' I asked.

'Er, nothing,' he said, quickly adding, 'Hey, what about your twin? What's she auditioning for?'

'I don't, I mean, she doesn't know yet.'

Flynn laughed (making my heart thud a little faster). 'That's right. I remember when the school inspector visited a few years ago and we had to sing the school hymn. Perse's voice was so bad that Principal Moody told her to mime.'

Suddenly, my heart slammed against my chest and lay there, lifeless and numb. The rainbow-coloured spirals behind Flynn stopped spinning and the song, *Be Mine*, which had been playing inside my head, ground to a scratchy, screechy halt.

I'd forgotten about the school hymn fiasco. After all, my life is littered with deeply scarring singing disasters. I can't be expected to remember them all. Flynn laughing at me was the final straw, and I burst into tears. Totally embarrassed, I ducked my head and scurried away as fast as I could so Flynn wouldn't see.

'Hey, where are you going?' he said. 'Auditions are that way.'

When I didn't answer, he called after me, 'Well, good luck, Portia! See you in there.'

I wanted to tell him I was Persephone, not Portia, but I was too busy scurrying. I bolted into the girls' toilets, locked myself in this cubicle, slammed the toilet lid down, wiped it with paper (just in case) and slumped onto the seat. After doing some serious ujjayi breathing, I calmed down enough to write this.

(If there are any splash marks or smudges on these pages it's from the rain, not my tears, I swear.)

Uh-oh, someone's calling me. Why can't everyone leave me alone?

Tuesday 16 February. 3:21 pm.
Back porch.

I raced home to write up the rest of today's events, as I'm totally bursting with the news. Today was definitely a rollercoaster ride, full of ups and downs.

To rewind, I'd locked myself in the loo and lost track of how long I'd been in there feeling sorry for myself after Flynn laughed at me.

I heard Jolie's voice and saw her mud-splattered shoes below the door.

'Perse? You in there?'

When I turned the lock and poked my head out, Jolie pounced on me. She steered me outside, telling me she'd been looking for me everywhere. The rain had stopped and the sun was stretching spindly rays through the clouds.

I glanced at the hall, scared.

'Miss Tamarind sent me to find you,' Jolie said. 'Auditions are almost over. You'd better hurry.'

'I'm not going,' I said.

'Why not?'

When I shrugged, Jolie crossed her arms and said, 'Come on. Spill.'

Well, I couldn't stand it any longer. I'd bottled my feelings up for days. I had to tell someone. I thought maybe I could trust Jolie - hoped I could trust her - so I wailed, 'I can't sing! You've heard me. I'm the worst singer ever.'

Jolie sighed and did a major eye roll. 'Oh, Perse, there are worse singers than you. Just not in our class.'

Then she laughed and said she was only joking.

'Look, you might not win any singing awards, but you're not the only one. You should still try out because it will be fun.'

'Easy for you to say. You can sing,' I said.

'I'm just lucky Mum's a music teacher. Remember, she gave me voice training,' Jolie said. 'If you could hear my brother, Sam, sing you'd know just how ordinary my voice is. Compared to him, I sound like a sick bird.'

She flapped her arms and squawked. 'See? Totally sick!'

She was so funny, I giggled and asked her how she could be so honest about her singing.

'Because I'm so much older and wiser than you,' she joked.

(She's eleven already.)

Suddenly, I realised maybe I should be more like Jolie and learn to laugh at myself.

Then, without thinking, I blurted, 'Portia's

been such a pain. Sometimes I wish I didn't have a twin.'

Jolie was shocked. 'I can't believe you feel that way,' she told me. 'You're super lucky having a twin. Practically everyone else at school wants one, including me. You and Portia have just forgotten that what you have is totally special. Maybe it will be okay again soon.'

Jolie is so smart and insightful that I reckon she's right.

But, standing there ready to go into the audition, I stopped thinking about Portia and me and remembered I was still terrified.

'I'm not going in,' I said.

'Why?'

'Remember the school hymn fiasco, and how I had to mime it?'

'So did half the school,' she laughed. 'Don't you remember?'

When I shook my head, Jolie asked, 'Look, do you want to be a princess or not?'

'Doesn't every girl?' I asked.

Then she grabbed my arm and marched me toward the hall. 'Well you'd better hurry up while you still have the chance.'

Hang on. Portia alert!

Exhausted. Sprawled on my bed.

That took longer than expected! Not only did Portia come in and interrupt my diarising, Mum came home early ranting about 'the art exhibition of the year' (her words, not mine), so I couldn't sneak off to do more writing.

Mum cooked mushroom and asparagus pie (a combination of my two least favourite vegetables), which was GROSS. I was forced to eat it because Mr Divine was having dinner with us for the second time in three days. Hmmm.

Mr Divine seemed to like the food, although he is rather thin so maybe he's in need of home-cooked meals. He sure complimented Mum enough. Every time he did, Portia sent me SECRET SIGNALS that said, 'Do something!' or 'Can you believe this guy?'

Even worse, she kept mentioning Dad in totally unsubtle ways, like, 'When did you and Dad first meet, Mum?' and 'Can we have a look at your wedding photos later?'

Mr Divine and Mum swapped a few SECRET SIGNALS themselves until Mum said, quite snarly, 'I think you're under the impression your father still cares about us, Portia.'

That sure stopped Portia in her tracks. I was pretty shocked too. When Portia asked her what she meant, Mum tucked her hair behind her ear and said, 'Forget it. I shouldn't have said anything.'

Tension with a capital T filled the room. Portia had managed to rile Mum good and proper. Thankfully, dinner ended and I sought refuge on my bed.

So, back to the auditions...

When I snuck into the hall, I saw Miss Tamarind sitting in a chair near the stage and Grace, one of the girls in my class, auditioning. Portia was sitting on the floor with Caitlin and everyone else.

As Jolie and I sat with them, I waved to Miss Tamarind. She shot me a not-so-secret-but-rather-angry signal of disapproval, which I pretended not to notice.

Portia was in a total panic. She pulled me close and asked me where I'd been, making out that I'd left her all alone. Well, alone except for the twenty or so other kids in our class, but I knew what she meant. Without Portia's constant babble sometimes I feel alone too. We're used to each other.

Trying to act casual, I whispered that I'd been busy.

'Doing what?' she snapped.

'Never mind,' I said. 'You auditioned yet?'

She nodded and I asked her how she went.

'I would have gone heaps better if you'd been here.'

'Since when do you need me?'

Portia rolled her eyes. 'Since, forever. You know I'm no good without you.'

I was totally shocked. Perfect Portia, who always acted so confident, needed me, Shy Persephone, to make her feel better.

'You kept raving on about how you were going to be the princess,' I said. 'You seemed sure of it. You certainly didn't say you needed me to help you.'

Portia flicked her hair. 'I know what I said. I was faking it. I thought you knew.'

'Nope,' I said louder than I intended. 'Totally missed that.'

'Perse!' hissed Miss Tamarind.

Portia and I covered our mouths to stifle twin giggles. For the first time in days, happiness whirled inside me. I thought, this is more like it, more like how being a twin should be.

When Grace finished (she was pretty good), Miss Tamarind called Flynn's name. His sneakers squeaked as he trudged up the steps to stand in the centre of the stage, his eyes kind of wild-looking.

'Which part are you auditioning for, Flynn?' Miss Tamarind asked.

'P-P-Prince Ch-Ch-Charming,' Flynn said.

Everyone laughed. (Kids can be so cruel sometimes.)

Miss Tamarind nodded, scribbled something on her clipboard, then told Flynn to start whenever he was ready.

Flynn opened his mouth to sing, but only air came out. He coughed and shuffled his feet. I held my breath, feeling so bad for Flynn I almost forgave him for laughing at me. Almost.

Flynn tried again. After a while, his voice rose to an almost-in-tune squeak, but he was obviously super nervous. When he finally finished, Miss Tamarind thanked him and he flew down the stairs and hid up the back of the hall.

'Persephone,' Miss Tamarind turned to me, 'glad you could join us.'

'Sorry, Miss.'

'Well, you're the only one left. Shall we see if you're as good as your twin?'

I grimaced, but Miss Tamarind missed it because she looked back down at her clipboard to pick up a piece of paper. 'I guess so,' I said.

She handed me the list of roles and asked which part I was trying out for.

As I clambered onto the stage, with shaking legs and trepidation-filled shoes, I scanned the list. Something caught my eye. Right down the bottom in tiny print. For some reason, I'd never noticed it before.

'Which part, Persephone?' Miss Tamarind asked again.

It takes guts to get up on stage and sing in front of people, and right then I knew there was no way I could do it. There was no way I could fill the role of the princess, or any other part, except maybe one; the one that was way down the bottom of the list, almost hiding, as if nobody wanted it.

'The narrator!' I said.

I heard someone ask, 'What's a narrator?'

'It's like a janitor,' someone else piped in.

Miss Tamarind blinked and said, 'Fantastic. For some reason every other girl wants to be the princess. Have you been practising something?'

'Uh, no.'

Miss Tamarind wound her fingers through her bead necklace (trying to be patient), and asked me if I knew any poems.

'Yes,' I said.

She waved her hand and said, 'Well, with confidence, please.'

I scratched my elbow, thinking. I knew loads

of poems, but now that I'd been asked to recite one, my brain froze.

Then, suddenly I remembered one. It was a poem Mum used to read to Portia and me when we were little, when Dad was still around and she wasn't too busy to spend time with us. I only hoped it wasn't too childish.

'Okay, ah, the poem is called *The Star*, by Jane Taylor,' I mumbled.

'Speak up, Perse,' shouted Miss Tamarind.

Several kids sniggered as I did some ujjayi breaths to calm my nerves. Then I began:

'Twinkle, twinkle, little star,
how I wonder what you are.
Up above the world so high,
like a diamond in the sky.'

'That's a baby song!' someone yelled.

'She's not even singing it!'

'Probably a good thing,' someone else sniggered.

Miss Tamarind told everyone to be quiet, and Portia growled at them to give me a chance. I shot Portia a SECRET SIGNAL of thanks and continued, nerves halting my words.

'When the b-blazing sun is gone,
when he nothing shines upon.
Then you show your little l-light,
twinkle, twinkle, all the n-n-night.'

My eyes flicked to the class as I continued, and I saw Portia mouthing the words with me. She remembered our poem!

I thought of all the times we had sat on the back steps or lay in bed after the light had been turned off, reciting the words together. I kept staring at Portia, watching her mouth form the words, like a mirror-image of me. The memories of Portia and me brought the words of the poem back so clearly in my mind that they began to form perfectly in my mouth. Instead of coming out tangled and messy, they started coming out clear and true. Watching Portia as I spoke, I even managed a smile.

'Then the traveller in the dark,
thanks you for your tiny spark.
He could not see which way to go,
if you did not twinkle so.

'In the dark blue sky you keep,
and often through my curtains peep.
For you never shut your eye,
'til the sun is in the sky.

As your bright and tiny spark,
lights the traveller in the dark.
Though I know not what you are,
Twinkle, twinkle, little star.'

When I finished, Portia was the first to clap. Everyone else joined in. Miss Tamarind cheered (I've never seen her so enthusiastic about anything I've ever done before) and said the part of the narrator was definitely mine.

Suddenly, the end-of-lunch bell clanged.

'For the rest of you, I will announce your parts tomorrow,' Miss Tamarind said, as we all got up.

Everyone (except me) groaned because they had to wait another day to find out which parts they got, but Miss Tamarind shooed them off to their next class.

So, I did it! I made it through the auditions and I'm going to be the narrator. Best of all, I don't have to sing. Tra-la-la! Phew!

PS: I've been writing so much my pen has almost run out. I'll buy a new one tomorrow.

I'm using my new gel pen (thought I'd try red for a change), which I bought after school this afternoon.

Well, Portia is mad, mad, mad! Miss Tamarind gave the part of the princess to Grace. I happen to think Grace is an excellent singer. Portia thinks otherwise. She wanted to submit a protest, but our gang convinced her that would be un-Grace-ious.

Still, I guess Portia must have really wanted the part of the princess. Instead, she's playing a beggar girl. She's so crushed that I actually feel sorry for her. I did try to make her feel better by saying that there was always next time, but she said she wanted to be a princess *this* time.

I'm sure she'll get over it, though. Portia always bounces back remarkably well.

I'd better go. I need a shower and dinner before Mum's yoga onslaught.

Watching Mr Pickleton wash his ute.

My top secret diary is top secret no more.
Yesterday, when I dropped my bag in my room
after school, it slipped out at the precise moment
that Portia walked in scoffing an orange.

I quickly stashed my diary back in my bag,
but it was too late. Portia shook her head and
laughed.

'What?' I said, acting innocent.

'What?' she said, imitating me.

We went back and forth like a tennis match.

'You're looking at me funny.'

'You're looking at me funny.'

'Were you looking at my book?'

'Your diary don't you mean?'

'What diary?'

'Uh, the diary you've been keeping since the eighth of February.'

When I asked her how she knew about my diary she said it was because she knew everything about me.

'You don't know everything,' I said.

'I know more than you realise. Besides, there isn't much to know anyway.'

Remaining calm, I asked whether she'd read my diary. She insisted she hadn't, but I wasn't sure whether to believe her or not.

'That's totally not like you,' I said.

'Well, it's totally not like you to keep secrets.'

I crossed my arms and insisted they weren't secrets, only thoughts.

'Secret thoughts,' she said, sounding a little hurt.

This was a surprise. I didn't think she would care that I was keeping a diary (except to snoop).

But I could sense, and see, that she was upset.

'I can have some privacy, you know,' I said, trying to be kind and firm all at the same time.

'I know,' she said. 'Look, Perse, you can have your diary. I won't read it, unless you want me to.'

'Honest?' I said.

'Honest. It does feel weird you keeping a diary when you've got me to talk to, but I understand. You need an alone activity, so that's cool.'

So now Portia knows about my diary but it doesn't matter. Another Phew!

Tuesday 15 March. 10:37 pm.
Super late, but I have to write.

Okay, so I haven't written in a while, which seems slack, but I've been so super Mum-like busy with school and learning my narrator lines and helping Mum organise her first-ever exhibition (which was tonight), that 'I haven't had time to scratch myself', as Gran would say.

We've just got home from Mum's exhibition, BTW. It went heaps better than expected, mainly because stacks of people from Mum's alternative therapy classes came and bought loads of paintings. At the end, Mum looked relieved and proud and happy. So did Mr Divine.

When we got home, Mum commented that her feng shui was finally paying off.

I asked whether we could afford to get the

roof fixed now.

'Darling, it means we can afford a lot of things.'

When Portia asked what she meant, Mum sighed and said, 'Well, it's difficult as a single mum trying to afford everything you girls need, especially when your father doesn't send any money.'

'Is that why you've been chewing your nails? Because you were worried about money?' I asked.

'It's not only the money. I've been worried about a lot of things,' she said.

'Like what?' Portia asked.

'Like how to raise two happy daughters and how to make people feel good about themselves and how to hold the warrior pose in yoga and how to cook the perfect borlotti bean moussaka.' She shrugged. 'Lots of things.'

I thought, with all her worrying, maybe Mum

and I were more alike than I realised.

Then she said something that surprised me.

'I was wrong to tell you that your dad doesn't care about you. He just has other things on his mind right now.'

We nodded, letting her know we understood.

'Besides,' she said, smiling now, 'my library of self-help books and the laughter therapy have shown me how to forgive your dad and to get on with my own life.'

'Does that mean dating Mr Divine?' asked Portia.

Mum choke-laughed and said it was awfully late for a school night and that we should get to bed so we'd be in a 'fit state' tomorrow.

That's why I'm writing under the covers, so Mum can't see the torchlight under the door. I'm yawning constantly though, so I'd better sign off.

Thursday 17 March. 9:20 pm.

Late, but not as late as last night.

T'was the night before the musical and all through the house... pandemonium erupted as Portia and I ran around like crazy geese trying on costumes and rehearsing our lines.

Well, Portia has only one speaking line, but she does have songs that she's had to learn. I, on the other hand, have loads of lines to remember. Just between us, I'm scaredy, scared, scared, scared!

Mrs Pickleton brought her sewing machine over earlier to finish our costumes. Mine is an emerald satin and taffeta ball gown. Portia's is a tacky brown - not caramel - dress with holes torn in it. She is playing a beggar girl, after all. Poor Portia.

Mum's attempt at making our costumes was disastrous and she ended up stomping around the house in a most unladylike manner. Worse still, Mr Divine chose that precise moment to arrive, so Mum was caught red-handed. Mr Divine just laughed, but Mum looked mortified: again.

Unlike Mum, Mrs Pickleton is a marvel with material and she 'saved the day', as Gran would say. It was worth putting up with Dill for two hours to have a properly stitched costume. (I thought I'd have to staple it together the way Mum was going.) I have decided, because she has been so marvellous, that I must remember not to nose-snort the next time Mrs Pickleton comes over in her aqua and purple yoga leotard. At least, I promise to try.

I must admit, I do look sophisticated and teenager-like in my gown and make-up, while Portia looks, well… like a filthy beggar girl.

Bet I don't sleep tonight. Did I mention that I'm scaredy, scared, scared, scared?

Friday 19 March. 8:07 am.

Eating rye toast smothered
with honey.

I was right, I didn't sleep at all. I tossed and turned and worried all night about being the narrator on a real stage. Oops, I don't have time to write any more, I've got to get to school.

I wish Dad could see us tonight.

Friday, 19 March. 5:45 pm.
Tucked in a corner
of the dressing room. Pre-show.

Madness and mayhem! You should see this place. It's like a zoo with all this screeching, squealing and squawking. I must write quickly. I don't have much time before we start.

Mr Divine drove us here. He drives way faster than Mum, BTW. Portia and I were so nervous about the musical that we couldn't speak. We just sat in the back clenching each other's hand.

Dad sent a text while we were on our way here. Although it was short, I was glad he remembered our big night!

'Good luck tonight girls! Knock em dead. Luv Dad,'

BTW, Mum looks BEAUTIFUL. She's wearing an actual dress, which makes it seem like a special occasion because she never wears dresses. She even bought a new necklace and matching earrings.

'Remember your ujjayi breathing,' Mum said, as Portia and I scurried backstage, 'and try not to be nervous.'

Easy for you to say, Mum!

I just came in here from backstage. Out there, kids were wandering around reciting their lines. Miss Tamarind and a few other teachers she'd roped in to help were flitting about, adjusting costumes and props. Principal Moody was flicking through music sheets and barking something about the piano needing tuning.

When Jolie saw me she wrapped me in a huge hug. 'I'm sooooooo nervous! How about you? You look great, by the way,' she said.

'Thanks,' I said. 'So do you.'

Jolie is playing Queen Zerla, Prince Charming's mother. She's wearing a ball gown like me, except hers is gold. She's also wearing a grey wig so she looks old.

Caitlin is a beggar girl like Portia and looks as raggedy as she does. From where I'm sitting, I can see the two of them nattering away like they haven't seen each other for a week. They don't seem the slightest bit upset about being beggars, even with black make-up smeared on their faces to make them look filthy. I knew Portia would bounce back well. That's one thing I do admire about her.

I can also see Flynn, laughing and joking with the boys. He's dressed in blue leggings, a blue velvet jacket and a white shirt with frills at the neck and cuffs. Some kids reckon he only got the role of Prince Charming because he's the tallest boy in class, but I think he's an okay singer when he isn't so nervous that he can't breathe properly and only makes squeaking sounds. Besides, he does look cute in leggings.

Oops. Miss Tamarind's calling me. Show's about to start. Wish me luck.

Saturday 20 March. 10:02 am.
Back steps, eating a cheese
and lettuce sandwich
(on wholemeal, of course).

It may be impossible to believe, but despite my pre-musical nerves I was fine when I got on the stage. It helped hugely that I knew my lines inside out and back to front. Even though I didn't play the princess or sing, I'm happy (and relieved) that I didn't make a total gooper of myself.

At the end of the show, the entire class (or, rather, the cast) went on stage to do the bowing and curtseying stuff. All the parents clapped wildly and camera flashes burst over and over, like tiny shooting stars. Portia was buzzing.

'Oh, Perse, this is how celebrities must feel!'

So I purred, 'Smile, dar-link!' in my best Hollywood accent. Portia and I laughed so much that Caitlin and Jolie asked what was going on.

'Just smile, dar-links!' I said. That set them off too.

When Portia and I ran down into the audience, Mum double-hugged us and said we were the best performers in the show - which she's meant to say, I know. She also mentioned that she'd taken some photos which she'd send to Dad.

Mr Divine said we were superb and asked if we'd like an organic, frozen yoghurt at YoYo afterwards? His shout. Portia and I said we'd prefer a non-organic, sugar-toxic ice-cream sundae at Iggy's Ice-creamery.

'Don't push it,' Mum said.

'Okay, we'd love a frozen yoghurt, thank you very much,' I said.

'Can Caitlin and Jolie come too?' asked Portia.

'Certainly,' said Mr Divine.

Then Portia turned to me and said, 'You were awesome, Perse. You didn't mess up once.'

'Thanks. You were great too.'

'I was okay,' Portia said, 'but you were terrific.'

'Because I didn't sing?' I asked.

'Well, there was that.' After a short pause she added, 'Only joking!'

'I know. I can take a joke.'

'Finally!' she said. 'But, really, I am sorry I gave you a hard time about your singing. I should have said sorry before.'

'Forget it. That was so long ago it's Egyptian history,' I said, not making a big deal of it - and feeling very mature in the process. Besides, seeing Portia in a brown - not caramel - dress was payment enough for her bad behaviour.

Then we jabbed each other with our matching

pointy elbows and giggled like totally together twins.

Right then, I realised that despite our differences, or maybe because of them, what Portia and I have is special. I don't mean being twins. I don't mean being sisters. I mean being twins and sisters and friends. It's something I wouldn't change for all the ice-cream at Iggy's.

'Well, Perse,' Mum said, 'I'm glad you found something you're good at, even though it isn't singing.'

Just to tease her I said, 'But, Mum, I am good at singing. You said I was.' Then I pouted, pretending I was about to burst into tears.

My acting must have been excellent, because Mum looked all flustery like she didn't know what to say, until I grinned and told her I was joking. Mum looked at Portia and sighed, 'Oh, that little sister of yours!'

We all laughed, except Mr Divine who looked confused, but Mum told him she would explain later.

'Come on, let's go find the others,' I said to Portia, taking her hand and leading her through the crowd to our friends.

Saturday 20 March. 9 pm.
In bed with my mind whirling
about everything!

So, the show is over and Portia and I are back to
being totally together twins.

I have been thinking about the things I share
as a twin, but this time I changed them around.

MY TOP FIVE BEST THINGS TO SHARE WITH MY TWIN ARE

1. Birthdays – as long as we get separate cakes.

2. A room – as long as Portia doesn't mess my side.

3. One mum – even though she's super-busy.

4. Friends – so we can all hang out together.

5. A face – because you don't need a mirror to see what you look like.

When I think about it, there are heaps more fantastic things about being a twin, like never being lonely and always having someone you can rely on and sharing clothes (well, the non-brown ones) and shoes and having someone who knows you better than anyone else in the whole world, even your mum.

Now I've run out of pages in my first ever NOT-SO-TOP-SECRET diary, so I have to make my writing small and squishy to fit on this last page. I'm off to buy another diary and maybe a new gel pen this afternoon (might try green this time) so that I can record my next totally terrific twin adventure.

TTYL!

Aleesah

Hi, I'm Aleesah, the author of this book.

I grew up in the country and had a lot of freedom as a nine-year-old. My older brother, my cousin and I would ride our bikes and go exploring, build cubbyhouses and billycarts, and rescue injured animals and birds. When I wasn't outdoors, I was usually curled up on my bed reading. It was quite an addiction for me and I often got into trouble for 'having my nose in a book'. I loved colouring in and won loads of prizes for my efforts. Quite shockingly, I also loved school!

I wrote stacks of stories and illustrated them with crazy stick figures. Like Perse, I kept a diary. And I can always remember desperately wishing I had an identical twin.

Serena

152

Hi, I'm Serena, the illustrator of this book.

I don't really look this freaky, but as an artist, I can make myself look as kooky as I like, and you need to be able to laugh at yourself sometimes.

I grew up in Melbourne with an older brother who taught me how to wrestle, an older sister who always had the coolest clothes and jewellery and a younger sister who enjoyed following me around everywhere!

I loved drawing, writing notes in my diary, dressing up our pet cat in dolls' clothes and creating mini adventures in our huge back yard. When I was nine years old, long socks were really cool, funny dresses with lots of frills and buttons were cool, straight hair was cool and even big teeth were cool... unfortunately I was not cool.

Other titles in the Totally Twins series.

www.totallytwins.com.au